Bermuda's
Sidney the Sail Boat
By Mark Booth

Illustrated by Patricia DeCosta

Designed by Daron Lowe

Published by
The Bermudian Publishing Company Limited
P.O. Box HM 283, Hamilton HM AX
Bermuda

Printed in Singapore

1994
First Edition
ISBN 976-8143-04-5

IT was a warm, sunny May
morning. Summer   was
coming. The sea birds knew it
and sang happy tunes to each
other and to themselves.

But Sidney wasn't happy. In fact he was completely fed up. It was just another day with nothing to look forward to for Sidney the Sail Boat.

Twice a day, the tide came in around him and lifted him up off the seabed and let him drift around in a small circle, held in the same position by his anchor and rusty chain, and twice a day he would get a sinking feeling as the tide turned and started to go out. So, slowly but surely, he was lowered back down into the soft, sticky mud.

ACROSS Hamilton Harbour Sidney could see a passenger liner called the 'Prince William' cruise majestically the last mile towards the dock along Front Street. A thin line of smoke drifted from its large blue funnel and three small, but powerful tug boats buzzed busily around the hull like bees around a flower, carefully guiding the magnificent ship into its resting place. Sidney looked on with envy.

"*Why me?*" he thought. "*I should be the one sailing across oceans, looking for new islands and chasing pirate ships or racing other boats and winning prizes.*" Sidney liked to dream, but really he knew that it could never come true because he was only twenty feet long and eight feet at his widest point with a wooden mast and a small cabin.

NOT far away, in deeper water, Rebecca was moored. She was a much bigger sail boat with a tall, shiny metal mast and pure white paint which reflected the sun. Sidney thought she was lovely and wished they could go out sailing together.

Rebecca could see that Sidney was upset so she called across to him. *"Cheer up Sidney, it's a lovely day."* *"It might be to you,"* he replied. *"Your captain takes you out every weekend, you know what it feels like to get the wind in your sails. You get washed and painted, but look at me, I've been dumped here for three months without moving."*

"**B**UT *you're for sale,*" said Rebecca, "*You haven't got a captain and a crew like I have.*" It was true. Sidney had a white sign nailed to him and on it in large letters, so that it could be seen from the boat club dock, it read "FOR SALE - WOODEN SAIL BOAT - VERY CHEAP - ENQUIRE AT CLUB OFFICE."

"I 'M sure someone will buy you soon,"* continued Rebecca sympathetically. *"I'm not,"* laughed a loud voice. It was Razor, a long sleek motor boat. He was painted bright red with two large eyes and a row of snarling white teeth looking menacingly forward from his bow. Razor was a racing boat and every weekend his two large engines would be started, then with a roar of noise, he would fly across the top of the water and out of the harbour into the open sea.

"BE quiet," shouted Sidney. *"I know that I'll be repaired soon and sailing again, then I'll show you what I can do,"* he said boldly. But in his heart, he wondered.

THE next day was Saturday and, as usual, Rebecca was being prepared by her crew to go out racing. *"I'll see you later,"* shouted Rebecca as her sails were raised and she started to move out into Hamilton Harbour. Sidney was still upset but replied as happily as he could *"Have fun and try and win for me."*

"So," thought Sidney to himself. *"Here I am, all alone again."* Razor had already left with a roar of engines and a long, loud blast on his horn.

BUT then he noticed a man who worked at the boat club pointing at him from the dock and next to him a rather strange looking person. The man had a sailor's cap on with white tufts of hair sprouting from its edges. He also had a long, white beard.

"I wonder what they want?" thought Sidney. *"They are probably laughing at me like everybody else."* But both men climbed down a ladder into a rowing boat and started moving toward him.

A FTER a few minutes, they reached Sidney and jumped on board. *"I can't see why you would be interested in this boat Captain Haggard,"* said the man from the boat club. *"I was going to get it broken up as it is in such a bad condition."*

Captain Haggard didn't say anything, he just started to move around Sidney, pulling on his ropes and banging his wooden sides, testing for rot. After a while, the men went below into the cabin.

FOR SALE

WOODEN SAILBOAT

VERY CHEAP

SIDNEY couldn't hear what they were saying but again he felt his sides being knocked and thumped all around. *"What is going on?"* wondered Sidney, getting excited; the Captain did seem interested in him. At that moment, the two men came back on deck and without a word, climbed back into the rowing boat and headed back to the dock. Sidney's heart sank. If the Captain didn't want him, the man from the boat club had said that he would be broken up and then as Razor had cruelly put it, all he would be was drift wood. *"I'll never sail again,"* thought Sidney, but little did he know this was very soon going to change.

SUDDENLY, the door to the boat club opened and Captain Haggard, this time alone, came out. He again climbed down into the rowing boat and headed back out towards Sidney. Sidney at first didn't notice the captain returning as he was feeling very sorry for himself and scared, but he finally saw him as he came alongside. *"He must have left something behind,"* thought a sad Sidney.

But, to Sidney's surprise, Captain Haggard climbed aboard and said *"Right Sidney, let's go sailing and see how you get on. I know you haven't been looked after very well, but if you get through this voyage, I will buy*

you and we can change all that."
Sidney couldn't believe what he
was hearing, he was so excited;
but this was going to be a test so
he also became very nervous.

The Captain prepared to set sail. Sidney's two canvas sails were brought on deck and attached to the mast and after pulling up the anchor, they were raised up into the air as high as they could go. Almost at once a gust of wind filled them and Sidney started to move forward. Sidney felt great. Finally, after such a long time, he was sailing again with the wind in his sails and the spray from the sea on his decks.

THEY headed out of Hamilton Harbour and into the Great Sound. At this point, the wind became stronger and waves bigger than in the sheltered harbour, but Sidney was doing very well and Captain Haggard steered him expertly. Sidney was beginning to become more confident and was enjoying himself, when disaster struck.

Suddenly, there was a loud
snap as one of the ropes which
held the mast upright broke, and
then another, and before
Captain Haggard could do
anything, the mast and the sails
came crashing down onto the
deck. Luckily, the falling mast
missed Captain Haggard but it
was a terrible mess with the
sails dragging in the water and
Sidney drifting hopelessly.

CAPTAIN Haggard pulled the sails back on board and sorted out the tangle of ropes, wood and sails as best he could, but he knew that help was needed to get them back to the safety of the harbour. There was only one thing to be done.

The Captain went below into the cabin and turned on the radio. *"May Day, May Day. Can anyone hear me?"* After a short silence, an answer came back *"Yes, we hear you. Have you a problem? Can we help?"* The relieved Captain Haggard replied *"Yes please. This is Captain Haggard on Sidney the Sail Boat calling. My mast has broken and I need a tow back into the harbour. I think I am about one*

mile north of Spanish Point."
"Okay Captain," came the reply.
"We aren't far away, we will be with you in a little while."
"Thank you very much," said a relieved Captain Haggard. *"Over and out."*

THE Captain went back on deck and looked around for his rescuers to arrive and soon, in the distance, he saw a bright object coming very quickly towards him. Sidney also saw it, and to his despair he realised it was Razor that was going to rescue him. How could he stand the embarrassment.

As Razor drew closer to Sidney, it seemed as if his smirking face, with rows of smiling teeth was even more mocking than usual. *"Need my help do you, drift wood?"* he called sarcastically. *"Well, enjoy the journey back as I think it might be your last."*

RAZOR'S crew threw a long rope to Captain Haggard. He caught it and tied it to the front of Sidney. *"Could you please tow us back to the Red Hole boat yard in the harbour?"* asked Captain Haggard. *"Sure thing,"* and with a roar of engines, Razor headed back toward the land with Sidney helplessly in tow behind.

AS they entered the harbour, they passed Rebecca who was cruising gracefully, through Two Rock Passage back to her mooring. She called to Sidney but even though he heard her he was too upset and embarrassed to answer. Also, he was scared. Captain Haggard said that this trip had been a test to see

whether he would buy him, and if he didn't he was going to be broken up. Well, Sidney could see only one possible answer. He had failed the test and now he was being towed to the boat yard where he would be smashed up into little pieces. His wooden sides trembled thinking about it.

RAZOR'S engines suddenly slowed down, as they approached land and Sidney saw a sign, "RED HOLE BOAT YARD - REPAIRS AND BREAKERS, NO JOB TOO LARGE OR TOO SMALL." Rebecca looked on sadly as Sidney was towed into position and pulled upwards out of the water by a big crane which hung above the boat yard and watched as Sidney disappeared from her view, behind a large shed.

OVER the next few days, Rebecca listened closely to the sounds coming from the boat yard. There was banging and hammering and sawing and it made Rebecca feel quite ill thinking what could be happening to little Sidney. Razor on the other hand just laughed. However, at the end of the week, all these noises suddenly stopped and instead only the sound of the crane, moving around to pick something up could be heard. As Rebecca and Razor watched, a beautiful little blue sail boat came swinging out from behind the boat yard shed.

"Surely, it can't be," growled Razor. *"Oh yes it can,"* cried Rebecca. *"It's Sidney."* And indeed it was. Sidney was lowered slowly and proudly back into the water. Sidney sighed with pleasure as once again he felt the water all around him.

HE had been so scared when he first had been taken to the boat yard but Captain Haggard had soon put him at ease. *"Don't worry, little Sidney,"* he had said. *"I'm not surprised that one of your ropes broke as you have been neglected for so long. All you need is a bit of work on you and you'll be a great little boat."* And, so it was. Sidney's hull had been painted bright blue and his deck pure white. The broken glass in his windows had all been replaced and, of course, he had finally been given all new ropes.

SIDNEY felt so proud as Captain Haggard raised his sails and they moved gracefully back to a new mooring between Rebecca and Razor. Despite everything, Sidney would sail again.

THE END

ISBN 976-8143-04-5

44